The Day
of the
Ogre
Kachinas

The Day
of the
Ogre
Kachinas

PEGGY D. SPENCE

Illustrations by
Janet Huntington Hammond

ROBERTS RINEHART PUBLISHERS
IN COOPERATION WITH
THE COUNCIL FOR INDIAN EDUCATION

Published in the United States by
Roberts Rinehart Publishers
Post Office Box 666
Niwot, Colorado 80544

Distributed in the
U.S. and Canada by
Publishers Group West

Published in Ireland by
Roberts Rinehart
Trinity House, Charleston Road
Ranelaigh, Dublin 6

The Council for Indian Education Series

THE COUNCIL FOR INDIAN EDUCATION is a non-profit organization devoted to teacher training and to the publication of materials to aid in Indian education. All books are selected by an Indian editorial board and are approved for use with Indian children. Proceeds are used for the publication of more books for Indian children. Roberts Rinehart Publishers copublishes select manuscripts to aid the Council for Indian Education in the distribution of these books to wider markets, to aid in the production of books, and to support the Council's educational programs.

INTRODUCTION

*T*HE HOPI INDIANS OF ARIZONA live on three flattop mountains called mesas. Some of their villages are almost a thousand years old.

Modern Hopi children go to school like other American boys and girls. They speak and write English, ride bicycles and play video games. They also learn the Hopi language, the history of the Hopi tribe, and the traditions followed by Hopis for hundreds of years.

One way they learn is through the *kachina* dancers and religious ceremonies held in the villages. Kachinas represent people, animals, and natural forces such as the sun and rain.

Hopi men make their costumes and paint their bodies as their ancestors did. The 'women' kachinas are really acted by men.

The kachina ceremony in the beginning of this story is part of a child's initiation into his or her mother's clan or family. The clan determines which religious ceremonies the child will take part in, which land he or she will use, and which kachinas the boys may become.

The Ogre Kachinas help the children learn right from wrong. Long ago, Ogres whipped children for their bad deeds. This story illustrates the ogre ceremony as it is practiced in most villages today.

*J*UDSON HONYOUTI WAS A HOPI INDIAN. He
wanted to follow the ways of his people,
but it was hard. Sometimes he was care-
less. Sometimes he forgot. And once in a while,
he lost his temper.

At such moments, he needed help from his
clan—help from his mother and father, his un-
cles and grandparents, and the village *kachinas*.

Judson was nine years old and no longer a *kekelt*, a hawk too young to fly. He was a member of his mother's clan. And he was old enough to know that the kachinas who visited the mesa were really men of the village. They dressed as the people and animals who had helped his ancestors so that he would learn to live the Hopi way.

Only a few months ago, he had sat with a group of boys in the kiva as the kachinas climbed down a wooden ladder into the large underground room. He watched silently as these heroes of Hopi history danced around the firepit.

4

They were dancing for him as he was wel-
comed into his mother's family. For him they
had painted their faces white and their bodies
yellow, blue, and red. For him they chanted
the songs of their grandfathers and whirled to
the music.

Suddenly, one of the dancers stopped before
Judson. In his hands were six feathered arrows
and a plain wooden bow. The dancer spoke only
to Judson.

"Once you were kekelt," the kachina said, "and we gave you a painted bow with marks to help you learn right from wrong. Now I give you a new bow. It is made of wood, but it has no marks to show you how to live."

Judson reached to take the bow, but his eyes never left the kachina's face.

The dancer continued solemnly, "You will make your own marks. You must choose for yourself what your life will be. If you want to become a kachina, you must follow the Hopi way. Think of others first, and take care of the earth. Hopis live in peace with people and with nature."

From that day, Judson tried to be a good Hopi, so he could one day take his place as one of the dancers. He helped his father dig water ditches to their cornfield. He threw rocks at the ravens to keep them away from the corn. He took care of his two little sisters.

Still, there were times when he needed help from his parents and his clan.

One morning, Judson was left to watch the sheep grazing below the red cliffs of the mesa. The sun was warm, and his eyelids dropped. The sea of curly wool swam before his eyes as they closed.

When his father's angry voice woke him, the sheep had scattered. Only two old ewes and their lambs still roamed nearby. Most of the flock had disappeared in the low cedar and juniper trees.

Judson and his father spent the rest of the day rounding up the stray sheep.

"The sheep are *pokmute*," said his angry father. "They help us. They give us meat, *sikwi*,

and wool for weaving. A Hopi cares for his animals before himself."

That evening Judson played outside his parents' cinder block house below the mesa. He shook a rattle his grandfather had made from a gourd and moved his feet to a chant he had learned in the kiva. He dipped and turned, raising his arms high as the kachinas did.

His mother appeared at the doorway. From the bowl she carried came the wonderful smell of mutton and hominy stew.

"Ummmmm," Judson said, rubbing his stomach. "*Knukquivi!*"

"This is for your grandfather," his mother said, smiling. "Only Grandfather loves knukquivi more than you. He will be waiting for his supper. Be careful now."

Stuffing his rattle in his jeans pocket, Judson took the covered bowl from his mother. The gravel road from his home to the top of the mesa was steep and rough, but Judson knew the trail by heart. His feet skimmed over the rocks until he neared the old part of the village.

Here he moved more slowly. The old flag-
stone houses seemed to sprout from the rock.
Near his grandfather's home, Judson felt the
spirits of long-ago Hopis around him. Juggling
the bowl in one hand, he quickly jerked the rattle from his pocket and give it a hard shake. The
bowl crashed to the ground.

"What is all this racket?" Grandfather asked,
stepping from his doorway.

Judson did not have to answer. His mother's bowl lay in shards. The village dogs lapped at the
mutton and hominy.

Judson knelt to pick
up the pieces. He

felt his grandfather's disappointment. He re-membered the kachina saying, "Hopis think first of others."

He told the old one, "I'll be right back."

Judson ran swiftly all the way home. But his steps were slow and sure as he carried his own supper back up the slope to his grandfather.

Later, as he lay in bed, Judson gazed at the wooden bow hanging on the wall. Twice in one day he had forgotten the Hopi way.

Then he remembered his grandfather smack-ing his lips while he ate the stew. He smiled,

glad he had given the old one pleasure, and fell asleep.

Early the next morning, Judson's mother asked him to build a fire for the *piki* stone.

"Today is swap day in the plaza," she explained. "I will make paper bread to trade for peaches and apricots."

Judson laid firewood under the large rock in one corner of the house's main room. Soon, tiny flames leaped and the black stone grew hot.

"Split more wood to keep the fire going," said Judson's mother. "Do not let the stone cool down."

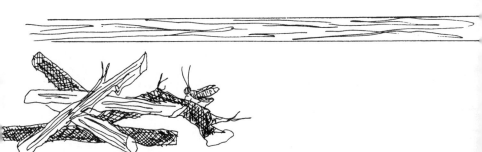

As Judson and his two small sisters watched, their mother mixed blue corn meal with water and added a pinch of ashes from the fire.

"That will keep the batter blue," she told her little audience, "and give the bread more flavor."

Then she greased the top of the polished rock with oil squeezed from watermelon seeds.

"And that will keep my piki from sticking," she said.

She dipped her right hand into the bowl and quickly spread the batter across the stone. As the thin, crisp sheets baked, she rolled them into tubes with her left hand and set them on mats to cool.

All morning she worked at the baking. Judson kept the fire going, while his sisters pretended to grind corn and make piki.

When the last roll of bread was done, Judson's mother gave one to each of the children.

"Do not touch the rest," she warned. "I must get ready to go to the plaza."

While his mother was in the other room, Judson tried to do as she said. But he was hungry, and the piki smelled so good. He took a handful of bread and began to eat. The tall stack of piki soon became very short.

"Oh, no!" his mother cried when she saw how little bread was left. "How can I trade for apricots with such a tiny bit of bread?"

"I'm sorry, Mother," Judson apologized.

"Something must be done," his mother said crossly. "Do you want to grow up to be a two-heart?"

Judson shook his head. He wanted to be a true Hopi, not an evil person.

With a sigh, his mother said, "The stone is still hot. Bring me more cornmeal."

Judson and his mother worked quickly. In another hour there was enough bread for trading.

"Now," said Judson's mother, motioning to the children. "Who will help me take this to the plaza?"

They all clamored to go. Once the piki was set out for other villagers to see, Judson took hold of his sisters' hands.

"Look!" he told them. " Baskets and pottery. Aren't the beads pretty? And there's a booth with candy."

Suddenly a shrill cry rang out. Metal clanged against metal. A noisy parade entered the plaza.

"Where are the children?" called a loud voice.

The Ogre Kachinas! though Judson, his heart beating wildly. The ogres have come to the village!

He put his arms around his little sisters. They clung to him and buried their faces against this legs.

Hands pushed Judson and his sisters forward. Soon they stood with a huddled group of boys and girls. Five dancers surrounded them.

Ogre Woman led the group. Her head was covered by a black mask. Her long matted black hair fell down over her face. A wide red-and-white mouth stretched from ear to ear. Yellow eyes glared at each child in turn.

"I'm searching for naughty children," the kachina shouted in a strange, high voice. "Hee-hee-hee-hee!"

Behind her, an ogre with a huge snout and sharp teeth scraped a saw against a stone wall, making Judson's skin crawl. Another monster clapped together the turtle shells strapped to his knees. Others clacked their huge bird beaks and slashed the air with yucca ships. They pointed to the baskets on their backs.

"Here!" Ogre Woman shoved a snare into Judson's hands. "Trap me a fat rabbit or two. Maybe then I won't put you in a basket for my supper!"

She gave snares and traps to all the boys. To the girls she gave dried ears of corn.

"In eight days I will come back," she screeched. If you do not listed to your parents, I will take you away. But if you are good, and grind lots of corn and catch lots of meat, MAYBE I will let your go. MAYBE!"

Swish! Swish! The *moho* whips sliced back and forth.

"Hee-hee-hee-hee-hee!" shrieked Ogre Woman, as the noisy parade left the plaza.

Judson remembered the ogres—they visited the village every winter. Would they take any children this time? Would they take *him*?

During the next week, Judson thought of the ogres often. He did his work at school. He helped his father mend the corral fence and the barn door.

But one day he grew tired of trying to be "good." He was tired of his sisters pestering him to play with them, so he kicked over their bone dolls. He slugged Brian Loma because Brian smeared mud on his face. And when Benny Talasentewa said he ran like a girl, Judson blacked his eye. He was no *mana*.

"Hopis are people of peace," his father scolded. "Our name, Hopi, means peace. You must not fight. Do you want the ogres to come for you?"

That night his father went to the kiva. Judson wanted to go, too, but he was not allowed.

"Not this time," said his father. "The men have much to talk about."

What would his father tell the ogres?

Judson thought about the stray sheep, the spilled knukquivi, and the paper bread. He knew he must catch many animals before the ogres returned.

He set his snare in the cornfield and caught two big rats. He trapped a rabbit by the well and four mice in the chicken pen. He cleaned his catches, frowning as he hung them from a stick. Would they be enough for the kachinas?

On the eighth day, a fist banged on the front door. An eerie metallic twang echoed through the house.

"Where is Judson Honyouti?" called Ogre Woman.

"He is here," Judson's mother answered. She gave Judson a gentle nudge.

Judson took up the stick loaded with the animals he would offer the monsters. Slowly he
stepped outside, and his parents followed.

"We like bad boys," one ogre growled. "We're
going to eat you up."

"Put him in my basket," yelled the other ogre.
The dancers surrounded around Judson and
his parents. They stamped their feet and

clacked their giant beaks. They whirled their whips and scraped their saws against the stones beside the road.

Above the clamor, his father's voice rang out. "What has our son done?"

"Judson Honyouti let the sheep stray," said Ogre Woman. "He wasted his grandfather's supper. He disobeyed his mother and ate her paper bread."

A long finger poked Judson's chest with each accusation. Judson hung his head. The ogres knew all he had done wrong. How could his mother and father defend him?

33

"And," said Ogre Woman, "he fights with other children."

The largest ogre stepped forward. Black eyes glared at Judson beneath a mop of white hair.

"You like to fight?" his voice boomed. "Fight me!"

"Leave my son alone," his mother's voice broke in. "He is not a bad boy. He has worked hard to get food for you. He has mice and rats and a rabbit."

Judson held up his stick so the ogre could see.

"I'd rather eat the boy!" thundered the monster.

"You do not want him," said Judson's father. "He is a good boy. He will make you sick if you eat him."

"How do we know you are not trying to trick us?" asked Ogre Woman.

"He does good in many ways," Judson's father continued. "He doesn't argue with his parents, and he is polite to old people. He even gave his own supper to his grandfather."

"He does not lie or steal," said his mother. "And he helped me make more bread to swap."

"Did he round up the sheep?" questioned one ogre.

"Yes," answered Judson's father.

"He is our son," said Judson's mother, "and we want to keep him. I will give you piki in his place."

She laid the paper bread in the monster's burden basket. Stepping back, she put an arm around Judson.

"And I will give you sikwi." Judson's father put a leg of mutton in the basket. He stood beside his son and put a hand on his shoulder.

Grumbling loudly, the ogres accepted the food. With beaks clattering and saws twanging, they moved down the road to another house.

Judson took a deep breath. His mother and father had given the kachinas piki and mutton and told them about his *good* behavior. As their parents did for them, Judson realized. As Hopis did a thousand years ago.

"Thank you, Mother," he said. "Thank you, Father."

In return, his parents smiled.

"Father?" Judson looked up, waiting.

"Yes, my son," his father said.

"Do you think I could . . ." Judson hesitated. "I mean, would it be okay if I take the sheep to the pasture tomorrow?"

His father laughed. "Can you stay awake this time?"

"I'm sure I can, Father," Judson replied confidently. "All I have to do is remember the kachinas." And how much his parents loved him, he thought to himself.

About the Author

PEGGY SPENCE has lived most of her adult life in Arizona where she teaches fifth and sixth grade in a small mountain town. An avid enthusiast of Native American culture and art, she has worked with children from many Arizona tribes.

About the Artist

JANET HUNTINGTON HAMMOND has illustrated books, greetings cards, menus, postcards, brochures, catalogs, and posters. She is an active outdoor peson and lives in Colorado.

If you liked *Ogre Kachinas*, you'll like other books in the Council For Indian Education Series. Roberts Rinehart publishes books for all ages, in the subjects of natural and cultural history. For more information about all of our books, please write or call for a catalog.

ROBERTS RINEHART PUBLISHERS
P.O. Box 666
Niwot, Colorado 80544
1-800-352-1985
In Colorado 303-652-2921